# The Diary of Dennis the MENACE
## Rollercoaster Riot!

Written by
Steven Butler

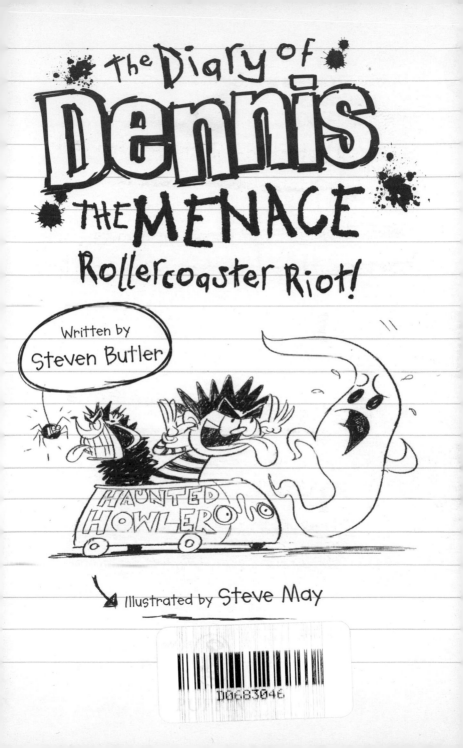

HAUNTED HOWLER

Illustrated by Steve May

PUFFIN BOOKS

Published by the Penguin Group

Penguin Books Ltd, 80 Strand, London WC2R 0RL, England
Penguin Group (USA) Inc., 375 Hudson Street, New York, New York 10014, USA
Penguin Group (Canada), 90 Eglinton Avenue East, Suite 700,
Toronto, Ontario, Canada M4P 2Y3 (a division of Pearson Penguin Canada Inc.)
Penguin Ireland, 25 St Stephen's Green, Dublin 2, Ireland (a division of Penguin Books Ltd)
Penguin Group (Australia), 707 Collins Street, Melbourne, Victoria 3008, Australia
(a division of Pearson Australia Group Pty Ltd)
Penguin Books India Pvt Ltd, 11 Community Centre,
Panchsheel Park, New Delhi – 110 017, India
Penguin Group (NZ), 67 Apollo Drive, Rosedale, Auckland 0632, New Zealand
(a division of Pearson New Zealand Ltd)
Penguin Books (South Africa) (Pty) Ltd, Block D, Rosebank Office Park,
181 Jan Smuts Avenue, Parktown North, Gauteng 2193, South Africa

Penguin Books Ltd, Registered Offices: 80 Strand, London WC2R 0RL, England

puffinbooks.com

First published 2014
001

Written by Steven Butler
Illustrated by Steve May
Copyright © DC Thomson & Co. Ltd, 2014
The Beano ® ©, Dennis the Menace ® © and associated characters
TM and © DC Thomson & Co. Ltd, 2014
All rights reserved

The moral right of the author, illustrator and copyright holders has been asserted

Set in Soupbone
Printed in Great Britain by Clays Ltd, St Ives plc

British Library Cataloguing in Publication Data
A CIP catalogue record for this book is available from the British Library

ISBN: 978–0–141–35574–0

www.greenpenguin.co.uk

MIX
Paper from
responsible sources
FSC
www.fsc.org
FSC™ C018179

Penguin Books is committed to a sustainable
future for our business, our readers and our
planet. This book is made from paper certified
by the Forest Stewardship Council.

# AAAAAAAAAAAAaGGGGGGHHHHHH!

This is . . .

THE MOST EXCITING THING . . .

I . . . I HAVE EVER . . .

I . . . I can't even . . .

I . . . I think my head might

explode!!!

# BREATHE, DENNIS,
## BREATHE!!!

# UGH!

I can barely write it down, my hands are shaking so much . . .

# HAVE A LOOK AT THIS!!

ARE YOU BRAVE ENOUGH TO TAKE ON

# THE HIGHEST, *TWISTIEST,* FASTEST ROLLERCOASTER

## THE WORLD HAS EVER SEEN?

Beanotown's own theme park,

## BEANOLAND,

is home to the newest, most terrifying
rollercoaster you can ride.

PUT YOUR COURAGE AND YOUR STOMACH TO THE TEST!

## OPENS THIS SUMMER!

I . . . I . . . can't believe it. I think I need to lie down for a minute . . .

## Note to self

← Breathe in

→ Breathe out

← Breathe in

→ Breathe out

← Breathe in

→ Breathe out

Phew . . . That's better. For a moment
I thought I was going to be sick or do a
**MEGA-FART** with excitement . . .
OR BOTH!!

(HA!) Nothing like this ever happens in
Beanotown . . . THE WORLD'S **BIGGEST
ROLLERCOASTER** and it's being
built at our own town's theme park. That's
the best news I've ever heard in the whole
universe . . . EVER!!! EVER!!! This is
going to be the brilliantest summer of my
life, I just know it.

But what am I doing??? I'm getting WAY
ahead of myself. The Vomit Comet doesn't
have its GRAND UNVEILING for another
few weeks and I've got loads to do before
then. I haven't even welcomed you all back
to the third book of my mega-menacing
manuals yet . . .

weee

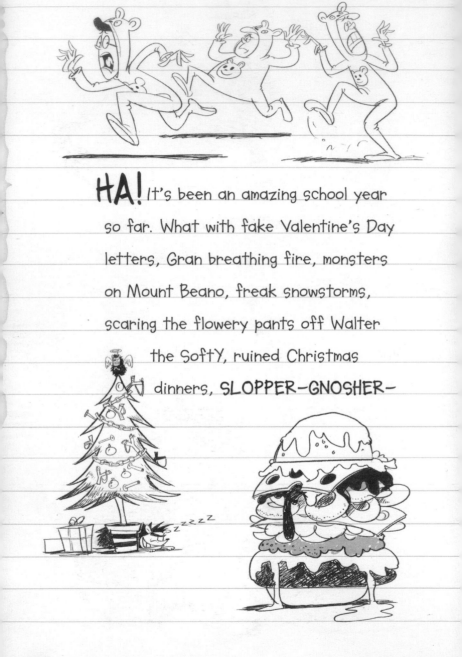

**HA!** It's been an amazing school year so far. What with fake Valentine's Day letters, Gran breathing fire, monsters on Mount Beano, freak snowstorms, scaring the flowery pants off Walter the SoftY, ruined Christmas dinners, SLOPPER-GNOSHER-

GUT–BUSTIN' BURGERS, haunted houses, midnight ice-cream feasts with Gnasher and **WHOPPING** great victories over hordes of flower-loving Softies, you'd think there couldn't possibly be anything to top it, right?

# WRONG!!

# Menacing Lesson no. (4672:)

There's always a better menace to be had out there. **Never stop looking** and be ready when the moment comes.

~~~~~~~~~~~~~~

Back at the beginning of the school year, when my crusty booky, **BUM-FACE** of a teacher gave me these diaries to write as a punishment for not doing my homework, I thought it was the worst thing that had ever happened in my life.

## BUT! NOW I LOVE MY MENACING MANUAL and I can't wait to fill it with new menacing secrets that will make Mrs Creecher wet herself with shock when she reads them.

(HA!)

I can't believe we're already on the **third** book of my menacing manuals. If you've been reading them right from the start of my first diary, you must be a pretty well-trained Menace by now.

GOOD JOB FOR MAKING IT THIS FAR!

(BUT) . . . if you haven't, there are a few basics we need to go over before we get much further.

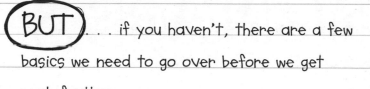

It's time for . . .

DRUM ROLL,
PLEASE!!

# FIRST . . .

# THE PERFECT MENACE

Make sure you've always got your trusty pea-shooter and catapult handy. You never know when you'll need it.

Messy hair. A good Menace NEVER combs it!

Unbrushed teeth, to help make your burps extra stinky on their way out.

Pockets stuffed with menacing supplies. Perfect for EVERY menacing occasion.

Stripy clothing. Think of it as your menacing uniform.

A good Menace always has a dog for a bestest-best pal. Abyssinian wire-haired tripe hounds like Gnasher are the best.

# A MENACE'S GREATEST NEMESES

A proper Menace has three

natural enemies:

## GROWN-UPS,

## TEACHERS

### AND

# SOFTIES!!

Each one is worse than the last

and all are EXTREMELY

# BORING!!

**RIGHT!** Now we've got the basics out of the way, I'd say it's time to crack on.

# BUT!!

Unfortunately, I've got some **bad news . . .**

Tomorrow is the first day of the summer term.

# YUP!

It's back to the great big ball of boredom that is Bash Street School for the third time this school year.

Normally, I'd be devastated . . .

Well, who wouldn't be? After all, school is full
of teachers and books and **SOFTIES!!!!**
It's the worst place on the whole planet . . .
But don't panic! Because now I can't wait to
get back there. The quicker I get back to
school, the quicker the weeks will pass and
Beanoland will unveil its newest rollercoaster,
and I'll be able to ride **THE VOMIT COMET!!**

**Right** . . . I'm off to bed to hurry the whole
thing along. It's only midnight, but I suppose
even Menaces need to go to
bed early sometimes.

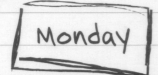

## Monday

**8.30 a.m.: Ugh!** What a rubbish start to the day . . . I only made it out of the garden gate before I spotted my arch-enemy Walter and his Softy chums, Bertie and Dudley, skipping about on the corner of our street. No one should have to look at those **SMARMERS** first thing in the morning!

Anyway, I thought I'd grab the chance to make my first menace of the new term, so I sneaked up behind them. I was just about to jump out and scare them when I heard what they were talking about . . .

OH BUMMM!!!

They're right . . . I totally forgot about that. On the last day of term, Mrs Creecher gave us mountains of boring worksheets to read about all kinds of history for a special first-day-of-term test.

BE OFF WI' YER!

18.

What was I supposed
to do with all those bits
of paper? I couldn't have
them cluttering up the tree
house and getting in the
way of my top—secret
menacing! So I squished
them all up with my spit
and used them as ammo for
my pea—shooter. **IT WAS
GREAT!** By the end of the
first week of the holiday, I'd
managed to write my name in
dried spitballs on the side of
the Colonel's house. HA!

BRILLIANT!

**9.45 a.m.:** Looks like old Whingey-Pants-Walter was right. Mrs Creecher has just announced we're having the history test **NOW!!!** It's just one torturous thing after another in this place. As if a test isn't bad enough on its own, first we had to listen to Headmaster waffle on about this and that and such-and-such in morning assembly before having our brains filled up with boring history.

# GAH!
## HISTORY!?!?

I don't care if Romans had elbows or if
Genghis Khan liked orange squash . . . It's
all SO boring! I don't know what the poor
Menaces of long ago used to get up to. It
must have been **SO AWFUL** to live in
a time before Mega-Zap Guns, Slopper-
Gnosher-Gut-Bustin' Burgers and
**BEANOLAND!!** UGH! It's enough to send
a judder all the way down your spine.

One thing's for sure . . . my ancestors
certainly didn't have as much fun as us
modern Menaces . . . Poor things . . .

MAXI-MENACE
CAESAR

NEANDER-MENACE

22

TUTANKHA-MENACE

KING MENACE VIII

Those poor Menaces must have been
bored out of their brains . . .

But why should I worry about some RUBBISH history test? I know loads of history . . . and . . . what more could I need to know about other than my **AMAZING MENACING ANCESTORS**? All the rest is **BORING!**

My ancestors of yester-menace wouldn't have worried about a stupid test. They'd have just fed gristly old Creecher to the lions. **HA!** Tutankha-Menace would have mummified his teacher if she'd even breathed the word 'TEST'.

Though it is quite handy that I'm a **WHOPPING GREAT GENIUS**. Mrs Creecher won't get one over on me . . . I'll ace it . . . just you watch.

## BASH STREET

### First-day-of-term History Test

Mrs Creecher's Class
Student Name: DENNIS

1. Who was Queen Elizabeth I?

That chubby lady off the telly . . . The one
with a face like a foot, who sang on that
programme and got famous.

2. Which country did the Romans come from?

# ROMANIA!

3. Name a play by William Shakespeare.

~~Romeo and Janet~~

Romeo and ~~Beverly~~

# ROMEO AND THE GIANT KILLER STINKBUGS FROM MARS! ✗

4. Where are the pyramids and who built them?

They're just behind Beanotown Burgers and I built them with Curly and Pie Face out of old baked-bean cans.

5. Who was Boudicca?

Mrs Creecher's great-grandma . . .

6. King Henry VIII had six wives.
Can you name them?

Hilda

Gertrude

Nelly

Maureen

**BUM-FACE!**

and **TERRY!**

*Detention, Dennis!*

**3.15 p.m.:**

**AAAAND** it's all happening like clockwork. **NOTHING EVER CHANGES** around here. Since I started at Bash Street School, I always get detention on the first day of term.

# IT'S SO UNFAIR!

OK, I made up a few answers on my history test, but they were almost right . . . almost. Creecher has always got her beady, vulture eyes on me and, when she hasn't, **WALTER– WET–PANTS** is always skipping off to tell her what I'm up to. It makes menacing pretty tricky at times . . .

Anyway, Creecher blew her bonce as usual and made me stay after school. Now I'm sitting in the classroom pretending to read history books while my two best menacing mates, Curly and Pie Face, are off playing secret agents in Beanotown junkyard. I'd be a **BRILLIANT** secret agent!!

I SHOULD BE THERE TOO,

DEFEATING GROWN-UPS AND

SOFTIES ON ALL SIDES WITH MY

TRUSTY CATAPULT!

If I wasn't such a well-trained Menace, I'd probably be dead from <u>**BOREDOM**</u> by now. Thank goodness for trusty **Menacing Lesson no. 5831!**

**Menacing Lesson no. 5831:**

There's no time like the present. The minute your teacher turns her back, jump into action.

**ESPECIALLY IN DETENTION!!**

**3.30 p.m.:** Waiting . . .

**3.35 p.m.:** Still waiting . . .

**3.45 p.m.:**

**Right!** Mrs Creecher has just wandered off to the school stock cupboard to get more chalk and staples and other teachery things. I think I'll have a bit of a rummage through her desk and see if I can find anything to eat.

**I'M STARVING!** The school canteen was closed because of a rat inspection today (they never found any – those rats must be super-smart creatures and don't just eat any old slop cooked up by the dinner ladies!).

Luckily, a good Menace knows that all teachers have got bags and bags of boiled sweets hidden in their desk drawers. It's a mystery why they do. I think it's all that teachers eat. Trust me. You keep looking and you'll find 'em . . .

33

> ***I . . . I . . . I WAS ONLY LOOKING FOR SWEETS . . .*** B . . . B . . . But I have just discovered something that will blow your socks off!

At first, all I found was a load of empty sweetie packets . . . yep! Mrs Creecher certainly gets through a lot of Extra-Crunch-Jaw-Jammers! They're the super-sticky-and-sour ones that get stuck in your teeth and to the roof of your mouth.

No wonder the booky bum-face always looks like she's sucking on something sour . . . **SHE REALLY IS!** She hadn't left a single one for her poor detention victims, though . . . It's so cruel!

Then there were poems to a man named
Archibald . . . <u>YUCK!</u>

*Roses are red,*
*Violets are fair,*
*Oh, Archie, I don't mind*
*you're losing your hair!*

*Your round belly's lovely,*
*Your pimples? Divine!*
*Oh, come smooch me quick!!*
*Please say you'll be mine!*

That's the most disgusting thing I've
ever read **IN MY LIFE**. Ugh! Why are
adults so **MUSHY?** Imagine smooching old
**SLOBBERCHOPS CREECHER!?!?**

# BLLEEAAUUCCHH!!

I nearly gave up looking . . . but then I found this! The most awesome, **BRILLIANTEST** thing of all. It's a letter from Headmaster to all of the Bash Street School teachers . . .

# LOOK!

# BASH  STREET

To all teachers at Bash Street School,

Here is prior notice of something very exciting. I'm sure you've heard by now about the brand-new rollercoaster that's being built at Beanoland theme park, the Vomit Comet.

The nice manager of Beanoland has offered to let a Bash Street School pupil be the first person in the world to ride it. I suggest we hold a competition to select the most deserving child. I'll announce it in tomorrow morning's assembly.

*Mr De Testa*

Headmaster

AAAAAAAAAAAAGGGGGGHHHHH!

I HAVE TO BE THE

FIRST PERSON IN

THE WORLD TO RIDE

THE VOMIT COMET!

Can you imagine it,
my merry band of Menaces?

# ME!

THE FIRST PERSON

IN HISTORY TO WHIZZ

ROUND THE TWISTS

AND TURNS AND

LOOP-DE-LOOPS

OF THE COOLEST

ROLLERCOASTER IN

THE UNIVERSE?!?!

I'd be the envy of all prankmaster generals everywhere . . . EVERYWHERE!

Whatever that competition is, **I HAVE TO WIN IT!** It's got to be something menacey and **BRILLIANT**, it just has to. Something like . . . umm . . . who can do the best skateboard tricks? Or . . . who can belch the loudest?

I would <u>definitely</u> win that!

# CHH!!

Only a competition like that would be worthy of such an **AMAZING** prize. I can't wait to hear what it is . . . I know I can win it!!

I bet the Vomit Comet is **MEGA**. I bet it has the highest drops and the twistiest turns. **Amazing!** I can't wait to see it. It's all I can think about!

(ARTIST'S IMPRESSION)

If it's anything like the rest of Beanoland, then it has to be **BRILLIANT**. It's one of the best places in all of Beanotown and for good reason . . .

BEANOLAND
IS
MENACE-TASTIC!!

It's the perfect Menace's playground, full of opportunities to have fun, make loads of noise and cause a bit of chaos. Me and the gang went there almost every weekend last summer.

Since I'm bound to win the competition and be the first person in the world to ride the new rollercoaster, I think I'll give you a bit of a guided tour in preparation for the big day. Come on . . . . I'll tell you all about the best bits.

**Behind those gates is the**

NOISIEST,

BUSIEST,

FUNNEST

PLACE YOU'LL EVER SEE . . .

There are parades with acrobats and jugglers
and HILARIOUS CLOWNS!

There are loads of brilliant fast-food
stalls like . . .

Not a vegetable in sight . . . Menaces can
stuff themselves silly with all kinds of yummy,
unhealthy things . . . GREAT!

There are all the **BRILLIANT, EXCITING** rides . . . ONLY A TRUE MENACE CAN STOMACH THEM!

# BUT BE WARNED!

Beanoland is also a magnet for **SOFTIES**. There are **RUBBISH** rides for **SCAREDY-CATS** and **WIMPS**.

## SOFTIES LOVE RIDES

## LIKE THESE!!

## A REAL MENACE WOULD

## NEVER GO ON THEM!!

The Lazy Lily Pads

The Sleepy Slides

**4 P.M.:**

**PHEW!!!** That was close! Creecher nearly caught me rummaging through her desk drawer, but I was too quick. The second I heard her **CLIPPY-CLOPPY** shoes coming back towards the classroom, I stuffed Headmaster's letter into my diary and jumped back to pretending to read all those history books. **Ha!**

Right, I'm off home for some dinner and to spend some quality time with my best pet-pal, Gnasher. I'm teaching him to poo in Dad's slippers. He's not quite got the hang of it just yet . . .

I don't think I've ever written these words before, but . . .

## Tuesday

### 6.30 a.m.:

I'M AWAKE!! YES! I set my Mega–Bleep–Digi–Clock to wake me up super early so that

I can be REALLY,

REALLY

READY

before I go to assembly, win the competition and become the FIRST PERSON IN THE WORLD EVER to ride

THE VOMIT COMET!

I've even written a speech for the big moment . . .

# Dear friends, teachers and **bum-faces!**

I'd like to thank you all for trying to beat me today, but there can only be one Dennis the Menace and I'm him! I'll think of you all when I'm whizzing above your heads on the best rollercoaster in the world.

## THE BEST ROLLERCOASTER IN THE WORLD THAT YOU CAN'T RIDE . . . BECAUSE YOU'RE ALL BUM-FACES!

Thank you.

**8 a.m.:** I arrived at school early for the first time in my life. **AGH!** I'm SO ready to win this. I even biked past Beanoland on my way here to have a look at how the Vomit Comet's shaping up. You can't see much over the fences except lots of cranes and scaffolding. BUT. . . !! Somewhere underneath all of that is **THE COOLEST ROLLERCOASTER RIDE OF MY LIFE**

. . . my stomach-churning destiny.

**8.25 a.m.:** CHECK . . . CHECK . . . OVER . . . This is DENNIS THE MENACE reporting live from Bash Street School. Here goes, my Trainee Menaces. We're about to head off to assembly. I can't wait to hear what the competition is going to be! I'll keep you posted . . .

# WHAT!?!?

## THIS CAN'T BE HAPPENING!

This is the worst day ever in the history of
Worst Days for Menaces.

The competition is . . . is . . .

### UGH!

I feel sick . . .

## GET A GRIP, DENNIS!

The competition is . . .

A BOOK

REPORT

COMPETITION!!

A BOOK REPORT?!!!!!?

I'm not even joking. There we all were, sitting in the school hall with Headmaster pacing around at the front, when he just said it . . .

**HE JUST SAID IT!! HAS HE GONE BONKERS?** We have to write a report about our favourite book, and the best report wins!

HOW CAN I WRITE A REPORT ABOUT MY FAVOURITE BOOK WHEN I'VE NEVER READ ONE IN MY LIFE? EVER!

Menaces don't _read_ books. They tear them up into little bits and fire them from pea-shooters or feed them to their dogs.

Only booky, boring husks of people read books. People like Walt.

 OH NO!

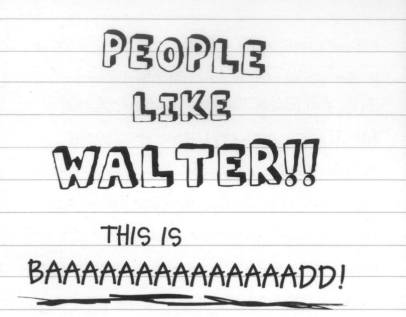

# PEOPLE LIKE WALTER!!

## THIS IS BAAAAAAAAAAAAAADD!

Everything has gone wrong and Walter has become the most likely person to win the chance to ride the Vomit Comet first. Headmaster has done this on purpose, I just know it!

It can't happen.

Can you imagine it? Dennis the Menace,
**THE PRANKMASTER GENERAL,
THE INTERNATIONAL MENACE OF
MYSTERY,** standing in the crowd while
Walter—Whinge—Bottom flies round the tracks
of the bestest, newest rollercoaster in the
world! What would people think if he beats me?
I'd never be able to show my face in town again.
I'd be stripped of all my menacing points . . .
No one would fear the name of Dennis the
Menace again! Not even teachers . . . Not even
parents . . . **NOT EVEN SOFTIES!**

It's time to get thinking, my Trainee Menaces.
I have one week to figure out a way of beating
my arch—enemy before the book reports are
collected and the winner is chosen.

**Come on, Dennis** . . . It's just a book. All you have to do is read one book. Just one stupid book and write a load of boring stuff about it. If I pick the most boring book I can find and only write about the most boring bits, Headmaster is sure to love it. After all, he **LOVES** anything that's dull and brain-numbing.

Better get organized . . .

# TO DO:

1. Go to Beanotown Library

2. Look at books

3. Pick a book

4. Look in book

5. Read book

6. Write book report

7. Win competition

8. Laugh in Walter's

**smarmy**

**BUM-FACE**

Midnight:

I can't sleep. Every time I close my eyes, I have library nightmares. I keep waking up sweating and screaming! All those books, and quiet and books, and shushing and **BOOKS** . . .

It's so awful!

This is going to be the trickiest quest I've ever faced . . . Brace yourselves, Trainee Menaces.

## Wednesday

~~Heading to Beanotown Library today to pick out a book and read it.~~

Was going to head to the library and pick out my book for the report, but it looked like it might rain . . . and . . . I had to wash my hair . . . and . . . I had to head straight home after school because of . . . umm . . . stuff! I'll go to the library tomorrow . . .

## Thursday

~~Definitely going down to Beanotown Library after school today and I'm **DEFINITELY** getting a book and reading it!~~

Couldn't go to the library today because of . . . umm . . . well . . . **I JUST COULDN'T, ALL RIGHT!?!?**

**7.30 p.m.:** What am I doing? If I don't get a book and read it, I can't write a report about it. And if I don't write a report then Walter will win the competition for certain! I heard him and his Softy sidekicks talking in the school canteen today.

I'm writing a report on my favourite book, *Little Bunny Bobkin and his Fwopsy Forest Friends*.

It's a WINNER!

Spiffo!

EL SNOBBO CAVIAR

I don't understand . . . I want to win this competition more than anything in the world, but every time I think about going to Beanotown Library and having to look through all those books I get a strange feeling in my stomach. It's like a gurgly, whooshy groan . . . It's the same feeling you get on the last day of the summer holidays or right before you go in to see the dentist. I think . . . I think I might be . . .

## ~~SCARED.~~

NO! I'M NOT WRITING IT . . .

Dennis the Menace isn't ~~SCARED~~ of

anything. **NOT OF ANYTHING AT ALL!!**

Especially a lot of dusty old books and loads

of massive words and killer, blood-sucking

librarians . . . and . . .

## WAIT A MINUTE . . .
# I'M A GENIUS!!

What was I thinking? I don't need to risk

my life and menacing reputation going into

Beanotown Library.

I don't need to read a book at all! I'll write a report about my own made-up story and just pretend I read it in a book. **HEADMASTER WILL NEVER KNOW THE DIFFERENCE!!** If I fill it with loads of action and adventure, it's bound to beat Wet-Pants-Walter's Bunny Bobkin report. **HA!**

# I CAN'T LOSE!!!

# ROBOTIC BRAIN-EATING PIRANHAS FROM MARS!!

A book report by Dennis

## I LOVE READING! LOVE, LOVE, LOVE IT!

Books are the best things in all the universe and the best book out of them all is *Robotic Brain-eating Piranhas From Mars!!* by the very, very, VERY famous writer Chris P. Bogey.

Anyone who hasn't heard of him is probably really stupid!

I really like the beginning bit when the thing happens about the thing, and that other part when the things go to that thing and get all of those things to save the thing. That bit was

## MEGA!

The middle bit was OK, but the BEST bit was the end when the Robotic Brain-eating Piranhas from Mars swarm into Mrs Creecher's house and eat her, but then spit her back out again because she tastes like old farts and scabby feet!

AND THEY ALL LIVED HAPPILY EVER AFTER!

## THE END

**PS** Did I mention I love BOOKS AND READING? I think I should probably win this competition just because of how many squillions of books I've read.

That'll do it . . . I can almost smell victory in the air. I'll just hand it in at school tomorrow and there'll be nothing left to worry about.

# BRILLIANT!

Friday

I handed my book report in . . . **AGH! I CAN'T WAIT TO WIN!!**

Walter looked so pleased with himself when he gave Headmaster his report on *Bunny Bobkin*. **Ugh! BORING!** Then he skipped off to scribble in his own diary about how clever and amazing he is. **SERIOUSLY!**

He wasn't even supposed to do a diary. When he found out that Mrs Creecher was making me write one, he cried and begged to have one too. He's such a **BUM-FACE!**

Anyway, enough about Walter. If I write any more about him, my menacing manual will start to smell like **BUM** . . .

Me, Curly and Pie Face are planning to head to Beanoland tomorrow to look at the Vomit Comet from up close. I'm so excited I could

**BURST** . . .

## Saturday

9 a.m.:

**UGH!** MY PLANS ARE RUINED! I was supposed to go and have a day of menacing fun with the boys today, but Mum and Dad insist they're taking me and my little sister Bea to the beach at Beanotown-on-Sea . . . **YAWN!!** Mum says it's healthy for us . . . **RUBBISH!**

Don't get me wrong, I **LOVE** the seaside . . . But Beanotown-on-Sea is just a big snoozefest. Especially when you compare it to how **AMAZING** Beanoland is!

It's not the cool, seasidey-type place
with surfing, arcade games, mountains of
candy-floss and sticks of rock to poke your
little sister with and then snack on later.
NOPE . . . it's the sleepy, no-fun kind of
seasidey-type place, full of snoring oldies in
deckchairs who smell of wee and bug spray.

I think it's going to be a long day . . .

Lunchtime:

**WOW!** How wrong was I!? Today has turned out to be the most fun I've had in **AGES** . . . I don't even mind that I didn't get to go and look at the Vomit Comet . . . AND . . . it's all because of my **BRILLIANT,** menacing sister, Bea!!

It started out **REALLY BORING!**

At **10 a.m.** we walked from one end of the promenade to the other.

At **10.15** we walked all the way back again.

78

At **10.30** we watched a seagull eating a newspaper filled with soggy old chips that someone had left on a bench . . .

WHO LEAVES THEIR CHIPS FOR THE SEAGULLS?? UGH! NOW I WANT CHIPS!!

At **10.40** me and Bea went to look for hermit crabs in the rock pools, but there weren't any. They must have got bored like us and gone somewhere else.

## BUT THEN!

At **10.45** I gave up all hope and decided to build a sandcastle. Can you imagine my misery? The prankmaster general forced to make a sandcastle!?!? Anyway . . . I had just finished when . . .   PFFFFFFFTTTT!!!!

A really strong gust of wind came
out of nowhere and exploded it.
ACTUALLY

# EXPLODED

MY SANDCASTLE!!

I didn't think anything of it at first
until I smelled the whiff afterwards.

I'd know that
stink anywhere!

# It was BEA!!

There she was, standing a little way off, with the look of a proud Menace on her face.

Before I knew it, it had become the **BEST** game ever. By the end of the day, she'd perfected her aim and we were exploding sandcastles from one end of the beach to the other. The snoring oldies in their deckchairs didn't know what had hit them. HA!!

POP!

Little sisters are pretty handy things to have around sometimes . . .

## Tuesday

Today's the day . . . It's been a week since Headmaster set us the task of writing book reports and today's the day I WIN and become the

COOLEST MENACE
IN THE WORLD!

84

BUNNY BOBKIN

I can't believe Walter still thinks he's going to beat me. I don't know why he even entered the competition . . . Softies **HATE** rollercoasters! Oh well, it won't matter soon anyway . . . Headmaster is announcing the winner in assembly . . . I'm off to celebrate my victory!

## The next Friday

**Noooooo!** *Nooooooo!*

It's all over, my Menacing Mates . . . I don't know how it happened.

# WALTER **WON** THE COMPETITION!!

# IT'S ALL WRONG!!

It started so well . . .

We all assembled in Bash Street School hall and Headmaster walked on to the stage holding my book report. (I recognized it from my drawing of Mrs Creecher being gobbled up by Robotic

Brain-eating Piranhas From Mars.) That was the moment I knew I'd won . . . The competition was in the bag and **THE PRANKMASTER GENERAL** was victorious once again.

But then . . . suddenly . . . Headmaster opened up his grouchy little mouth in front of everyone and said that the reports had to be on real books . . . so apparently I'm disqualified!

# ME!?
# DISQUALIFIED!!

How could it happen? My book report was by far the best. Who else wrote about teachers being chewed on by intergalactic, killer fish? IT'S NOT FAIR!!

It was so awful watching that Smarmy-Smarmer go up on stage to collect his special ticket.

Now Walter will get to ride the Vomit Comet first and . . . **EVEN WORSE!** Headmaster announced that the whole event is going to be shown on TV!! The entire world will be able to watch a Softy defeating the greatest Menace that ever lived. I'll never be able to show my face at Beanoland again . . . I suppose stupid Walter isn't quite as soft as I thought he was . . . who knew he liked rollercoasters? It's so unfair!

Well, that's my summer term ruined . . . What am I going to do now?

## Saturday

Today I scuffed my heels around the garden.

Then I stared at the wall for a few hours.

Then I lay face down on the floor and practised groaning to myself.

# AAAAAAAAAAAAGGGGGGGHHHHHH!

## Wednesday

Today I humphed to myself

 10,000 times . . .

Thursday

Today they made us draw and paint
our own silhouettes in art class. I
waited until everyone was gone and
added a few extra bits to Walter's
and Angel Face's pictures. Angel Face
is Headmaster's daughter! I really
thought that would cheer me up!

But it didn't make me feel better . . .

# MIGHTY MUMS

# *Ask Angela*

Dear Angela,

I have a terrible problem. Every time something good is about to happen in my life, a BUM-FACE goes and ruins it. I think there might be a plague of BUM-FACES and no one has noticed yet. What should I do? I thought about squishing the BUM–FACE, but I can't find a mallet big enough. I'm distraught . . .

Dear D of Beanotown,

Goodness, you sound so upset. I completely understand. I've never heard of the terrible Bum-Face Disease before, but I suggest you march your friend straight to the doctor for some cream to put on it. It's a terrible thing to have your face turn into a bottom and it should be looked at immediately. Does that help?

*Angela*

The next Monday

Today I drew skulls and

crossbones . . . lots of them.

## Tuesday

Today I pretended I was sick and stayed home from school. Then I sat under my duvet and didn't move for most of the day . . . **I DON'T UNDERSTAND WHAT'S HAPPENING!** I still can't believe that I lost out to Walter . . .

## WHAT'S WRONG WITH THE WORLD?

**COME ON, DENNIS!** I need to shake this off . . . even Gnasher has stopped wanting to play Fetch the Postman with me. Hmmmm . . .

# The next Wednesday

Ok, so it's a new day and I'm determined to have a good one. It's about time I stopped moping about and got my menaciness back in gear, and there's no better time to do it. Today is Bash Street School's sports day. If I can't beat Walter at riding the Vomit Comet first, at least I can beat him with a bit of sportiness.

**Menacing Lesson no. 4444:**
Menaces love a good run-around, but you mustn't waste your menacing energy. Never stop looking for a short cut . . . There is always an easier way to do things.

96

Unfortunately, I'm not allowed to take part in most of the activities . . . Oh wait . . . I haven't told you about that, have I? **Ha!**

## IT'S BRILLIANT!

Every year I come up with **GENIUS** new ways to win on sports day. **WELL, WHY NOT?** I can't use up all my menacing energy on running about like a headless Dennis, can I? That would be breaking the Menacing Code!

The not-so-great thing is that Headmaster always seems to catch me and bans me from doing it again . . . Each year I have to work harder to find different ways to win, Menace-style, because he's always got his eye on me.

There was the time I put Super–Sticky–
Fix–It–Glue on my spoon before the egg–
and–spoon race.

It worked perfectly until I won the race and waved my spoon in the air as I cheered. It didn't take Headmaster long to notice my egg wasn't going anywhere . . .

There was also the time I greased one end of the tug-of-war rope . . .

And the time I dug a
few teensy holes in the
running track . . .

Headmaster even banned Gran after she

took part in the parents' race . . . on her

## CHARLEY DAVIDSON!!

This year, the only thing I'm allowed to take part in is the long-distance running. They make us run back and forth and all around Beanotown - it's **SO BORING!** Headmaster thinks it

## Real Race Route

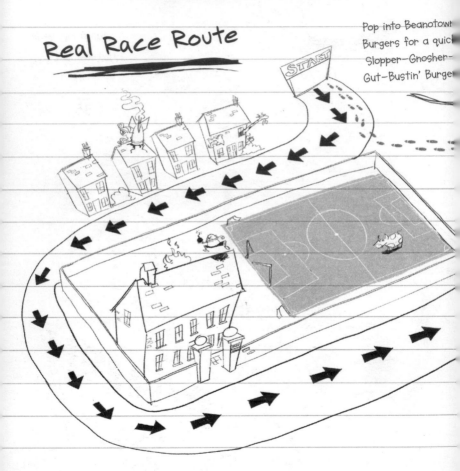

Pop into Beanotown Burgers for a quick Slopper-Gnosher-Gut-Bustin' Burger

will wear me out and I'll be too tired to be a Menace . . . **Ha!** I'll show him. I've got it all planned out . . .

Jump on the number 73 bus.

Get off the bus behind Mr Har Har's Joke Shop.

Join the race again.

FINISH

WIN!

# WOULD YOU BELIEVE IT!

That made me feel so much better. There's
nothing like a good menace to cheer you up.
AND . . . there's no chance of Headmaster
finding out. He's WAY too lazy to follow me
round the entire course. **BRILLIANT!**
Beating Walter and seeing the disappointment
on his **BUM-FACE** when he realized he
hadn't won the race was just what I needed . . .
Ahhh, the simple joys of menacing!

Something very fishy is going on . . .
It's not long now until the big unveiling
of the Vomit Comet at Beanoland and
Walter has been wafting around the
school for days, waving his special
ticket about to make sure that
everyone sees. Anyway . . . that's not
the fishy bit . . .

This is . . . In the playground at
playtime, I noticed Walter and his
cronies sitting on a bench at the edge
of the footy field and Walter was
looking like he was about to burst into
tears. I sneaked up behind them, hid
behind a tree and had a listen . . .

Call me crazy, but I think Walter was talking about rollercoasters . . . He was describing 'horrible, fast, clattery things' and saying how much he hates them! **What's going on?**

**10.30 p.m.:** I can't stop thinking about what Walter said to his crybaby cronies today. I just have to know what's going on and the only way to do that is to get my hands on Walter's diary. Shouldn't be too much longer before Mum and Dad are asleep . . .

**10.50 p.m.:**

# CHECK . . .
## CHECK . . .
### OVER!

This is Secret Agent Dennis reporting for duty. I've just sneaked out to the garden and retrieved Dad's fishing rod from the shed. With a bit of Secret-Agentiness, it shouldn't be too hard to grab Walter's diary. Better get over to his house sharpish . . .

**10.55 p.m.:** YES! We're in luck, my Trainee Menaces. With all this hot weather we've been having, Walter's left his window open. All I have to do now is hook his diary out of the window and make off with it before anyone notices me.

**11.13 p.m.:** Still trying! This is harder than I thought . . .

**11.17 p.m.:** Any time soon . . . If I keep at it, I've got to get the diary eventually . . .

**11.26 p.m.:**

GOT IT!!!!

Ok . . . it might be late at night, but **I HAVE TO KNOW WHAT'S GOING ON** . . . Let's see what he's written . . .

My dearest Diary,

Today I went to the supermarket with Mumsie to buy fresh smoked salmon for my darling cat, Claudius. Oh, how I love strolling through the organic vegetable section. Such a rainbow of rooty beauty!

BORING!

My best, darling Diary,

How I've missed you today. I had a ferociously exciting time at the Beanotown Library today. Someone spoke in a voice that was louder than a whisper. It was CRAZY!!! I was practically shaking afterwards . . .

Dearest, dearest Diary dear,

I'm in such a pickle. I just don't know what to do. I entered a competition at school to win a chance to be the first person to ride on some ghastly rollercoaster. I only entered because I didn't want that awful Dennis to win. He's such a rapscallion, I tell you. Anyhow, something just frightful has happened. I won! Now they're expecting me to go ~~         '~~ thing. I'm petrified! I want to give the ticket away, but I refuse to give it to a Menace. The trouble is none of the Softies I know will go on it. I need to find one who will. What am I going to do?

# I KNEW IT!

I knew that snarky little snitch-brain didn't like rollercoasters. He's done this just to get at ME! **WELL, I'LL GET HIM BACK!!** I'll figure out a way to make that **WHINGEY BUM-FACE** sorry . . .

So he's planning to give the ticket away to a Softy that likes rollercoasters . . . **FAT CHANCE!** There isn't a Softy alive that would happily set foot on a fast ride . . . Well, not unless . . .

The greatest plan that's ever been dreamed up by a Menace has just popped into my head. Ha! This is going to be the greatest moment of my menacing history. MENACES OF THE FUTURE WILL TALK ABOUT THIS FOR CENTURIES TO COME . . .

I've got work to do!

## Friday

I'm already putting my plan into action. There's no time to waste if I'm going to be in with a chance of getting that special ticket and being the first to ride the Vomit Comet.

**12.30 p.m.:** Every day at 12.30 when the bell rings and everyone goes to the school canteen for lunch, the school secretary leaves her office to go and eat her sandwich and drink her grown-up coffee drinks in the staffroom. This always takes her about ten minutes, which gives me just enough time to sneak in and type up a quick letter.

Walter's always off crawling round Mrs Creecher when we're in class. It should be easy to slip the letter into his school bag before the end of the day.

Dear Walter,

As the maturest, cleverest and all-round ~~BUM-FACIEST~~ BESTEST pupil at Bash Street School, I'd like you to meet and welcome a guest of mine when he arrives in Beanotown tomorrow. I'm too busy trimming my nose hair to meet him myself. He is a young pupil from . . . ummm . . . SAINT POSHLY'S SCHOOL FOR THE MEGA-RICH . . . called . . . erm . . . Gordon Guffington-Smythe and he is visiting for the day. I'd love you to meet him in front of the town hall at 10.30 a.m. and show him around and make him feel right at home. I'm sure you will both be great friends.

Thank you,

The Mayor of Beanotown

# MISSION ACCOMPLISHED!

I managed to get the letter into Walter's bag
when he was giving Mrs Creecher an origami
flower he'd made her . . . **UGH!**

Now I just have to wait for him to read it . . .

**3.30 p.m.: BINGO!!** The bell just rang
and I saw Walter reading the letter as he
was walking out of the school gates.
He won't be able to resist a chance to smarm
up to the Mayor.

Yikes . . . I've got work to do before tomorrow.

# OPERATION BECOME A SOFTY

First things first. If I'm going to fool Walter into thinking I'm a Softy and get that ticket from him, I have to be really convincing. It's lucky that I'm a Master of Disguise, my Menacing Students.

But . . . to be really convincing, I'm going to need more than just a change of clothes. A poodle is the perfect Softy pet! Sorry, Gnasher . . .

Gnasher wasn't happy, but he soon changed his mind when I promised him a whopping great **TREAT** if he plays along. He's the **BEST** dog ever! I'll think of some way to reward him later. For now I've got some serious pooch pruning to do.

**5 p.m.:** With a bit of patience and Dad's ear-hair trimmers, I think it's worked a treat. Meet Gordon Guffington-Smythe's pet poodle, Princess . . . **Ha!**

Hmmm . . . Now me . . . I think it's time to raid Dad's wardrobe and see what I can come up with for the morning. This is going to be fun!

## Saturday

**7 a.m.:** Thanks to my trusty Mega-Bleep-Digi-Clock, I'm up bright and early and ready to transform myself into the poshest, richest, most boring Softy there's ever been. Walter will be begging me to be his best friend in no time . . .

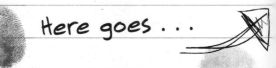

Here goes . . .

**10.25 a.m.:** I'm outside the town hall. It's so strange . . . Everyone looks at you differently when you're a Softy. It's like they're not afraid of me any more. **WEIRD!**

Walter is never late so he should be here any sec . . . **OH . . . HE'S COMING! HA!**

Wish me luck!!

Sunday

**9.05 a.m.:** MY MERRY BAND OF MENACES, I HAVE ONE QUESTION FOR YOU . . .

WHO IS THE GREATEST

**MENACE**

IN THE LAND?

# I DID IT!

Walter is giving his ticket to Gordon
Guffington-Smythe!! **THAT'S ME!!** My top-
secret plan was a complete success . . . Ugh!
I certainly had to work for it, though. Today
was a battlefield of boring. You wouldn't believe
what torture I had to go through to get it . . .

I knew it was going to be a tough day from the minute Walter arrived.

We went everywhere! **EVERYWHERE!!!**
Well . . . everywhere except anywhere fun.
Who knew there were so many boring places in
Beanotown? It's like a whole new side of home
that I never even knew existed!!

Walter dragged us round the museum . . .

Then there were the Beanotown Gardens . . .

We watched the ducks on the pond in

Beanotown Park . . .

Listened to opera at the theatre. It was

SO LONG AND BORING!! Something called

*The Magic Tuba!*

WE ATE VEGETARIAN FOOD! YES, YOU READ IT RIGHT . . . I ACTUALLY HAD TO EAT VEGETABLES!! (And Gnasher too!)

And then there was the sleepover . . . I had to meet Bertie and Dudley and spend a whole night with them on Walter's living-room floor. It was torture . . . **TORTURE!** They were wearing their **TEDDY BEAR ONESIES!**

Gnasher nearly blew it when all those veggies from earlier started BUBBLING up in his doggy tum. Before I could stop him, he let rip the biggest gassy guff and inflated our sleeping bag! Who would have imagined a 'Princess' could smell so bad? Luckily, Walter believed me when I blamed the symphony of parps on dopey Dudley! I love it when an unexpected menace comes together!

This morning, just when I thought I couldn't take it any more, I came out with the killer question. I just had to or I would have lost my brain to **BOREDOM ROT!!** In my poshest, pansiest Gordon Guffington-Smythe voice, I asked him if there happened to be any rollercoasters nearby because I 'absolutely love them, golly-gosh'.

And that's when he said it!! It worked! Right there and then, Walter offered me his special ticket to ride the Vomit Comet . . . He looked so relieved I thought he was going to cry at first. **Ha!**

The grand unveiling at Beanoland is in **TWO HOURS** and I'm going to be the first person to ride it!!

I just have to keep up this Gordon Guffington rubbish for a little bit longer and I'll claim my title as the **GREATEST MENACE IN THE UNIVERSE!**

I don't think Gnasher is quite as happy as me, but he certainly cheered up after I gave him extra helpings of Double Fatties' double-fat ice cream when we got home . . . It is a celebration after all!

**AND WE'RE OFF**, my fellow Menaces. What a strange term it's been so far . . . It's all been worth it, though. Just thinking about riding the Vomit Comet is enough to make any true Menace happier than a Menace has ever been before.

I'm meeting Walter at the Beanoland gates at 11.30 this morning. I'd better crack on and turn myself back into Gordon again. Whoever would have guessed that a Softy could be so useful to a Menace?

**12 noon: GAH!** Well, we arrived in Beanoland, but we found out the Vomit Comet unveiling isn't for another two hours. That means I have to spend EVEN MORE time with Walter and his cronies wafting around on the Softy rides . . .

> Let's ride the Lazy Lily Pads!

**1 p.m.: AGH! I'M GOING CRAZY!** We
went round the Lazy Lily Pads again and again
and AGAIN for over an hour. IT'S SO BORING!
To make it even worse, Curly and Pie Face
walked past and nearly spotted me. I had to
yank Dad's blazer over my head just in case
they recognized me. **CAN YOU IMAGINE
THE SHAME?** Walter kept clapping and
giggling to himself like it was the most thrilling
thing that's ever happened to him. That Smarmy
McSmarmison is so annoying . . .

If I didn't want to ride the Vomit Comet
SO MUCH, I'd make Walter go on it just to
see his face . . . Ha! Can you imagine it? The
King of the Softies crying like a toddler as he
loop-de-loops his prissy pants off.

Not long now, Dennis . . . Not long now.

## 1.50 p.m.: THIS IS AMAZING!
## THE WHOLE OF BEANOTOWN HAS
## TURNED UP TO SEE THE LUCKY
## HOLDER OF THE SPECIAL TICKET
## TAKE THE FIRST RIDE! There are TV

cameras everywhere and I can see everyone I
know in the crowd. Even my amazing menacing
Gran has shown up! She'll be so proud of me
when she sees how I've tricked Walter in such a
clever way. When he hands over the ticket and

I reveal myself as Dennis, he'll be so angry that he's done something **GREAT** for a Menace, he'll probably poo his flowery pants.

# WOW!
## THE VOMIT COMET!

I can't wait to see it. There's a huge green curtain hiding it from the crowd as we speak. It's nearly time!

**2 p.m.:** Oooh . . . The manager of Beanoland has just walked on to the podium in front of the rollercoaster. He's about to pull the curtain down. **THIS IS IT!**

You should see it! The Vomit Comet is the most unbelievable thing I've ever seen. It's MASSIVE and it's mine for the riding.

The Beanoland manager made a speech and asked Walter to come up on stage. <u>Ha!</u> He was trembling like a flower in the path of my Rapid Reaper machine.

I've decided to give my ticket to my new dearest chum, Gordon Guffington-Smythe!

**2.45 p.m.:** That was hilarious, my Menacing Mates. I walked up to the podium and took a bow. No one recognized me! I even saw Headmaster in the crowd and he was staring straight at me without the slightest clue who I really was. It was my greatest moment ever.

I took the ticket from Walter, turned back to the crowd and then . . .

And it was right then that things got interesting. Everybody in the crowd gasped. Walter screamed and, before I could stop him, he made a lunge for the ticket. A Softy would **NEVER** tackle a Menace. He really, really, <u>**REALLY**</u> didn't want me to have it. I tried to jump out of the way, but Walter grabbed hold of my arm and wouldn't let go. He just kept screaming and flapping at me!

Just when I thought he was going to get the ticket, a massive gust of stinky wind knocked him away.

I looked up and saw Bea in the crowd, standing on Gran's shoulders. My amazing little sister had saved me!

I was just about to relax and head to the
front carriage of the Vomit Comet when
Headmaster and Mrs Creecher ran up on to the
podium, followed by Bertie and Dudley, shouting
that I couldn't have the ticket.

Come
back!

You little
Menace!

I ATE VEGETABLES TO GET
MY HANDS ON THAT THING AND I
WASN'T ABOUT TO LET IT GO NOW!

So . . . I RAN!

Now, my Trainee Menaces . . . I can't
wait to tell you this last part.

# IT'S THE FUNNIEST

## THING THAT HAS EVER
## HAPPENED TO ME . . .

### EVER!

When I got to the rollercoaster
carriage, I jumped in at the front and,
before they realized what they had
done, all the Softies, Headmaster and
Creecher all piled in behind . . . all
except Walter. **Ha!** He tumbled in right
at the front next to me. And then there
was a big clicking sound and the safety
bars lowered on to our laps . . .

Do you know the one thing better than getting the first ride on the world's best rollercoaster? It's getting the first ride on the world's best rollercoaster with all your enemies pooing their pants in fear right there beside you ON TV!!! HA HA!! IT WAS BRILLIANT!!

WE WENT

UP ...

UP,

UP,

UP,

UP,

UP,

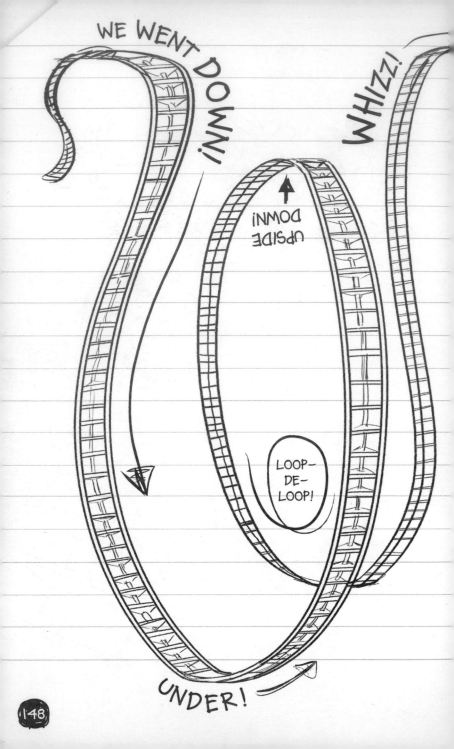

149

## Sunday evening

Ha! My Menacing Mates, that was **THE BEST** moment of my life **EVER!**

**ME!** Riding the WORLD'S **BIGGEST**, FASTEST, CRRRAAAZZZIIIEEESSSTTT ROLLERCOASTER FOR THE FIRST TIME WITH THE WORLD'S MOST BORING PEOPLE. Walter couldn't walk because his knees were trembling so badly afterwards.

Headmaster was in such a state of shock that they couldn't make him let go of the safety bar in the carriage. They had to take him home still in his seat.

Well, that's that for another long, boring school term. WASN'T IT GREAT!?!?

I suppose the moral of this story is . . .

# IF YOU CAN'T BEAT THEM JOIN THEM . . .

## AND THEN BEAT THEM!!!

## Friday, a week later

**BUT it's not over yet!**

There's one last thing I have to tell you about.

# IT'S MEGA!

So the last day of the summer term finally arrived and the big moment came when I had to hand my diary in for Mrs Creecher to read. I can't believe I managed to keep writing it for a whole school year.

Mrs Creecher still had a bug in her bonnet about being forced to ride **THE VOMIT COMET** and I could tell she was just itching to tell me off for not doing a diary.

She looked so shocked when I handed all those notebooks over. <u>HA!</u>

Anyway . . . she took them to her desk, settled herself down in her chair and . . .

DENNIS!

DON'T STOP MENACING!

BYE!!

# LOOK OUT FOR
## THE NEXT

# the Diary of
# Dennis
## the MENACE

## COMING FEBRUARY
## 2015!

# MENACE FUNNIES

## Laugh — or else!

Dennis tried squashing some cans of pop, but he had to stop.
**It was soda pressing!**

Dennis was getting a lift from Dad, but he couldn't remember how to fasten his seatbelt.
**Suddenly it clicked!**

Mum's making a reversible jumper for Dennis.
**He's looking forward to seeing how it turns out!**

Dennis made a wooden go-kart, with wooden wheels and a wooden seat.
**It wooden go!**

'Dennis, I'm late for work – can you call me a taxi?'
**'OK, Dad, if you insist – you're a taxi!'**

Dennis didn't always like his hair – **but it grew on him!**

Bea threw a can of pop at Dennis – **luckily it was a soft drink!**

# MINX MAYHEM

Minnie gets back on her bike every time she falls off.
**She always re-cycles!**

Minnie's learning to juggle.
**She's OK, but if she tries with more than three objects, things get out of hand!**

Minnie lost her temper while she was doing gymnastics.
**She completely flipped!**

Minnie visited Little Plum and ended up in charge of the whole tribe.
**She's a little miss-chief!**

Minnie was really annoyed when her parents didn't buy her the expensive rollerblades she wanted.
**What cheapskates!**

'Mum, how did you know I hadn't washed my face?'
'Easy, Minnie. You forgot to wet the soap this time!'

Minnie's best ever present was a set of drums.
**Every week, Dad gives her money not to play them!**

Minnie couldn't remember how to throw a boomerang.
**Eventually it came back to her!**

# The Bash Street Kids' Classroom Capers

Teacher: How can we keep the school clean?
Plug: By staying at home!

Sidney: Is it wrong to punish someone for something they haven't done?
Teacher: Of course it is!
Sidney: OK then. I haven't done my homework!

Teacher: Can anyone make up a
sentence using the word 'lettuce'?
Spotty: 'Lettuce' out of school early!

Why did Teacher have to
turn the lights on?
**Because his class was so dim!**

What happened to the
plant in maths class?
**It grew square roots!**

Why was the maths book
always unhappy?
**Because it had a lot
of problems!**

What did zero
say to eight?
**Nice belt!**

# Angel Face's
## NOT-REMOTELY-ANGELIC Laughs

Angel Face demanded a go at playing cricket.
**She was a big hit!**

Knock, knock!
Who's there?
Boo.
Boo who?
**Aw, don't cry – it's only me!**

Why are you wearing loud shoes?
**So that my feet won't fall asleep!**

What do you say to a hitchhiker with one leg?
**Hop in!**

What kind of hair do oceans have?
**Wavy!**

# COLLECT ALL THE BOOKS IN THE DIARY OF DENNIS THE MENACE SERIES!

## HAVE YOU GOT THEM ALL?

# IT'S PRANK TIME

Find out all about those pranks that went above and beyond the call of duty. The April Fool's Day gags, the hoaxes, the scams, the urban legends: they're all here, in one big beautiful package. Oh, and you get a stretchtastic catapult too, with two balls and a target!

## DON'T MISS IT!

# FIND DENNIS AND GNASHER IN . . .

Dennis and Gnasher are hiding from Mrs Creecher because Dennis hasn't done his homework. Find the pair in each spread, and prove you're smarter than a teacher!

# STICKY MAYHEM WITH THE BEANO GANG!

Packed to the rafters with puzzles, activities, funnies and over one thousand stickers of all your Beano favourites, from Dennis and Gnasher to Calamity James and the Bash Street Kids.